Fam and Other Natural Disasters

Anita Goveas

REFLEX PRESS

First published as a collection in 2020 by Reflex Press
Abingdon, Oxfordshire, OX14 3SY
www.reflex.press

Copyright © Anita Goveas

The right of Anita Goveas to be identified as the
author of this work has been asserted in accordance
with the Copyright Designs and Patents Act 1988.

All rights reserved. No part of this publication may be
reproduced, distributed, or transmitted in any form or
by any means, including photocopying, recording, or
other electronic or mechanical methods, without
the prior written permission of the publisher.

A CIP catalogue record of this book is
available from the British Library.

ISBN: 978-1-9161115-5-4

1 3 5 7 9 10 8 6 4 2

Printed and bound in Great Britain
by Imprint Digital

Cover image by Neilras/Shutterstock.com

www.reflex.press/families-and-other-natural-disasters/

To Steve, he knows why

CONTENTS

Fire

What Really Gets You Is the Rising Heat	11
A Pilgrimage Can Be One Way	13
Defeating the Demon	15

Water

Various Histories of Sea Serpents	21
Warning Systems	25
Finding Venkat	29

Wind

Turning into the Wind	35
Knowing the Answers	41
Let's Sing All the Swear Words We Know	45

Love

Monochrome	49
Magic and Candlelight	55
The Man in the Yellow Shirt	59

Families

Because Someone Else Dances	65
And Reverse	69
Virmala Nagra's Hypotheses on Marriage and Motherhood	71

Fire

What Really Gets You Is the Rising Heat

There's an ancient prophesy that you'll die by volcano. It's passed down to you at birth, like your grandmother's light eyes and your father's square chin.

It's not just your curse, others in your family succumbed to fire. Your great-grandmother was as happy at the birth of her daughters as at her sons. After the third girl was born, and her inability to learn proper values was firmly established, she went outside to fetch the rice pot from the cooking fire before it bubbled over. They worked out what happened from the quantity of ash.

On a school trip to Chislehurst Caves, a pale skinny boy in an ink-stained shirt whispers your hair is as dirty as coal. You lean your head against cool rock, and it starts to bubble around you. You avoid sitting on walls after that.

Things that can kill you: expectations, ignorance, other's people's hate. Longing.

Things that can be avoided: fate.

You're hard on things that draw heat: fridges, fans, air conditioners. When you're twenty-one, your new laptop explodes after a discussion with your tutor about Winston

Churchill and the West Bengal famine. You hide it at the back of a cupboard and write everything by hand.

Your aunt walked away from a marriage proposal from a man twice her age and her parent's refusal to send her to engineering college in Hyderabad, into a blazing sun. They found one singed brown chappal and a twisted earring. This happens in your lifetime.

They'll discover a dark slick that leads to your piled-up clothes, neat and unstained but smelling of hot tar and barbecue. They'll never be sure you didn't get the volcano first.

A Pilgrimage Can Be One Way

Packing list:

- 62 pairs of underwear (no chance to do laundry);
- two bras (might as well enjoy the zero-gravity);
- cotton trousers, T-shirts, shorts;
- one treadmill (zero-gravity great for elevation, not good for muscle-tone);
- one pair of shoes for the treadmill;
- spacesuit (just in case I have to do any after-launch repairs);
- space helmet (see above);
- space boots (ditto);
- 124 packets of dehydrated food (make sure it's heavy on the butter chicken), 62 bottles of water;
- dry soap, dry shampoo;
- toothbrush, toothpaste (although, in space no one can hear you scream... with toothache);
- *A Suitable Boy* by Vikram Seth (I should finally have time to finish it);

- Ravi Shankar's *Passages* for me, Norah Jones's *Little Broken Hearts* for Roopa;
- internet-enabled camera (those coronal storms are meant to be unforgettable);
- red sari, for the descent;
- Roopa's ashes;
- internet-enabled laptop, to send the last message to my family of crowdfunders and the well-wishers and the morbidly curious and the delighted trolls.

To do:

- add the course plotted by the engineering team to the memorial website, remembering the Venus gravity-assist;
- talk to the Gen X space team, make sure the PayPal transfer went through (19,188,600 rupees is a lot to process), and that Roopa's modifications to the carbon-carbon composite were properly made;
- practice talking to their doctor at the medical, explain again that even the Gods of technology need to be appeased sometimes, and a two-month journey alone is not much compared to five years plotting your own death;
- finish the speech for the last message: thanks to all who contributed to the first crowdfunded human sacrifice, no robot-driven probe could give the world this view of the sun, Roopa you were my life and my light.

Defeating the Demon

Charun is fidgeting because that boy never sat still a day in his life, but the rest of us are listening. Mum's always told the story of Rama coming back after defeating Ravana while she lights the diyas, but this is the boys' first Diwali with us, and they don't know how we do things. Their last one too, now their mum is better. She still looks tired, but her hair is brushed, and her big brown eyes are clear, not like the last time I saw her. She's my favourite Aunty-who's-not-really-an-Aunty, with her love of puns and her dangly earrings, and her husband Erish was my favourite Uncle-who's-not-really-an-Uncle, with his moustache as big as his laugh, so I get why him dropping dead knocked the wind out of her. Mum took her to Luton airport when she went back to Jaipur to rest. Promised her that looking after the boys for a few weeks was only payback for Aunty Tripta being one of the few friends from home who stuck around after my parents divorced and Mum drank a bit more than socially. Who'd have known that unwashed woman in mismatched shoes would be able to pick herself back up after 14 weeks?

It wasn't easy, going from being a mostly ignored only child to being a big sister overnight. Not that they wanted much looking after; I guess their mum had been zombified for a while, and they'd got used to looking after themselves. Charun had nightmares for the first few days, kept checking we all hadn't vanished while he was asleep, and that boy trips over anything including his own feet, so I got used to watching him. And Pranay needed time to work out how not to bump into everything in his wheelchair and got antsy if he hadn't baked anything for a while. We weren't much for cooking before they came to stay, which is why that whole peanuts in the mawa kachori thing is so weird. The boys said how much their dad loved peanuts, but we've never been much for stocking the cupboards, and I saw Mum do the shopping to make the sweets today myself: maida, pista, cardamom. Def no peanuts. I think Aunty Tripta might be allergic; she went so pale, kept touching her emerald necklace, and Mum is rubbish at telling the boys anything. She did her eye-smirky thing like it was funny.

I think Mum might be stressed. She'll want things to be perfect to welcome home her friend, and she's usually good at the little stuff, remembering what food people like, what they watch on the telly, if they're afraid of anything. She bought the boys and me blue T-shirts for the festive new clothes tradition, and she bought Aunty Tripta a bright green scarf, saying it was her favourite colour. But Pranay said to me it was their dad's favourite colour, and he loved to see Aunty Tripta in it. She's cut her hair off, stopped dyeing it, I guess because Uncle Erish liked it when she looked a certain way. It seems to me she doesn't want to be reminded of him too much, and I don't know why Mum hasn't realised that. Mum had a lot to do yesterday, spring cleaning, stringing the lights up outside, changing the boy's bedroom on the ground floor back to her office, she can't think of everything. Although, legend has it, she organised my Naming ceremony from her hospital bed recovering from the Caesarean, including choosing my clothes.

We're supposed to be going to the first ever Diwali Festival in Luton town centre, which is a BIG DEAL, but no one seems to be in a hurry. The boys are covered in evidence of stuffing themselves with crumbling samosas and sticky moti pak, we're all ignoring the crunchy, perfectly brown mawa kachori, Aunty Tripta's still playing with her necklace. Mum's usually running around, tidying everything and everybody about now, but she's getting out a photo album to show Aunty, something about remembering the first time she saw her in green. She's popped into her office, left the door open, and the sofa bed and the air mattress still seem to be in there. But she said she had something important to do before, when she shut herself away for ages. She's brandishing that album, and I recognise it; it's her wedding album. The one supposed to have been burnt the day my dad had a baby boy with his girlfriend. It all swims before me, the peanuts, the scarf, the photo album that would have pictures of her wedding day and a happy, smiling Tripta and Erish. I knew Mum always wanted a boy, but not how far she would go – you don't call your only child Krishna if you'd thought of any girl's names. Mum wants to keep the boys, and she's trying to piledrive through Aunty Tripta to do it. Rama needed help to defeat his demon. I sit next to Aunty Tripta, hold her hand. I whisper that we should go to the festival. She nods, and I hustle to get the boys ready. Her palm was sweaty, but I wipe mine on the new T-shirt mum bought, it seems dirty now. The boys crowd round their mum, and mine just stands there watching. The four of us go out the door, I can't resist slamming it, and Aunty Tripta laughs. She knew too. I've got used to the boys.

Maybe she'd like a houseguest.

Water

Various Histories of Sea Serpents

No one talks about what Nana keeps in the basement. You get used to the hollow thumping in the mornings, how she removes one worn chappal and bangs on the kitchen wall. You learn to put your whole focus, your whole being into the food you make together. Her appas are perfect, densely textured on the outside, hiding their sweetly slippery coconut centre.

Wriggling on your hard, narrow bed, sometimes you dream of twisting around frantically until you can hold your tail in your mouth. Rough ropes bind you because of your destructiveness, but you will cause your own ending. This is comforting, when the silence in the house makes you want to shed your skin. You scratch less at the pulse that jumps in your elbow, and the burning line between your budding breasts.

In history you learn of Ragnarok, the end of days. The walls of the classroom are full of tall, blonde heroes astride flaming boats and monstrous horses. Your drawing of Jormungandr, a black-haired, brown-eyed sinuous beauty who grows too big for the earth, lies in a drawer.

No one talks about why Nana has a basement. Apartment buildings flourish like palm fronds in Mumbai, fringed by corrugated iron shacks that people pass over. She looked out over toiling fishermen and angled trees, in broiling sun and roiling rain. In Kent, gardens are the treasure, the excuse to feel watery sun on parched skin. Your tired father and your ceaseless mother looked for eight months to find a house that Nana tolerated. One of her suitcases, tied up with blue string, was dripping. She never goes outside.

You fall asleep on the bus to sixth-form college and imagine shattering earthquakes and virulent winds. Sometimes, at home, you wake from your internal vortex to a tremoring floor that stretches you out and relieves internal pressures. The bed vibrates, the walls shake, the oval box on top of the cupboard where you keep your secrets rocks from side-to-side. At the edge of sound, there are chipping noises, tiny hammers or a persistent chappal.

You read a book about the Bakunawa, the dragons who cause earthquakes and eclipses. You loop yourself in bedsheets and stare down the moon. It can only ignore you, and you're used to that. You draw craters and shadows, dark streaks of volcanic crust. Nana helps you make the roundest idlis from pounded rice; they shine like pearls. You suck them down slowly as if you can swallow all your problems.

No one talks about why Nana needs her basement, or why you need Nana. The days you wrap up in blankets and can't get out of bed, the squeezing headaches, the time your mother had to leave the office as you'd wedged yourself under a sink in the girl's toilets. The itch, itch, itch along your spine as if your skin will fissure.

You have visions of tangled limbs in the bath, as warm liquid saturates you, holds you down along your fault lines. You're wrapped around the precious core of yourself, revealing this would bring untold disasters. There is a trial approaching, you can't hide from it, but you can prepare.

You find a picture of a Naga, the serpent race, in your Nana's handbag. It's speckled with droplets, forgotten raindrops or ancient tears. You remember, from a time before, that treasure can be protected with weapons like venomous knowledge and fierce belief in unbreakable connections. You draw your mother and Nana making sweet crescent-shaped almond cookies. You smile with your eyes as you draw in their tails.

Warning Systems

Four hours before: The first sign is deep in the earth, a tremble becoming a tremor. There is time to flee to higher ground.

Forty-nine-year-old Xavier Da Sousa leans back in his twenty-second-floor Canary Wharf office, sinking into his first Glenfiddich of the day. The slight tremor in his right hand causes drops of amber liquid to bounce off the edge of his Waterford crystal glass. He picks them up, one by one, with a wetted finger, the way his father chased grains of rice even in the throes of Parkinson's. He tastes earth and ash.

In the end he needn't have worried. He outlives them all.

Forty-five-year-old Elisabeth Da Sousa smiles through the aftershocks from her second-ever orgasm, enjoying the tremors rolling deep in her belly. The purple-haired woman sprawled across her runs a pale hand over her dimpled brown thighs. This newly discovered pleasure feels so undeserved she takes it as retribution that this is what she was doing as the wave gathered pace.

Eventually she dies alone in her Richmond garden flat, dreaming of a woman she can't name.

Two hours before: Then, water may recede from the coast, exposing the ocean floor, reefs and fish. Some escape routes may be cut off.

Twenty-two-year-old Mary Da Sousa drops the coral earrings she's borrowed from her mother into the sink at Café Rouge; an attempt at returning them to their original habitat. She throws her blue plastic hairnet in after, an expert at the right dramatic gesture to use before leaving a room. She takes the expression on her ex-manager's face and the clapping of her former co-workers as her due.

Ultimately, when she returns herself to the ocean ten years later in unnecessary sacrifice, it's only accompanied by the shushing of the waves.

Twenty-two-year-old Marcus Da Sousa scrubs the last piece of grime from the empty tropical fish tank that was the twins' joint twelfth birthday present. His father wanted to replace them, but it wouldn't have been the same. He talks to Maggie, the long-dead forktail rainbowfish, the way he always did when his bronchitis flared up. He talks about it the most after, the space that's left, he's even interviewed, holding back tears, on local TV.

So the painful way his lungs fill with water for the final time makes it into the papers; the son of the financial genius, the brother of a teenage mermaid.

Nineteen-year-old Magdalena Da Sousa, Maggie to her friends, lies back on the deserted white sand beach and puts in her headphones. It's how she's always dealt with the arguments she lives in, whether the voices in her house were too loud or too quiet, or when she needed to recharge. She's started *Their Eyes Were Watching God* in the middle and already read the last page, something that her brother, her favourite teacher, would frown about. She immerses herself in Janie Crawford's life.

She never knows she's exactly thirty minutes from solid ground.

Twenty-nine minutes before: An approaching tsunami creates a wall of water and loud 'roaring' sound similar to that of a train or jet aircraft, unmistakeable if you can hear it. Run.

Finding Venkat

It's difficult to know what the difference is between a family tradition and a routine bordering on insanity, but every summer we (the Agarwal family) go to the Oceanarium Bournemouth. Our number ebbs and flows. But we trek there from London and Leeds and Llandudno, by train and car and coach, rest up in fancy hotels or cheap B & Bs that provide free condoms. This year it's Daya and me. We study the feeding times, make a plan, we've never stuck to the map. We'll fit around the turtle feeding and the fish frenzy at Penguin Beach. And no family visit is complete without seeing the sharks. Venkat really loved whales, but sharks are the best Bournemouth can do.

Daya likes the clownfish. Because she's eleven years old, *Finding Nemo* has warped her brain, and she thinks they have personality. We skip past the Great Barrier Reef section; it's too soon. The Marine Research lab is new, not yet tainted by anything. We wiggle our fingers at seahorses and stare at spiky lionfish. Until Daya starts reading out in her thin, lisping voice how clownfish are female dominated but they all start out life as male, and it's too much to take in on an empty stomach.

We smile at the pig-nosed turtles on the way to the café. This is where Aunty Meena called me a little piggie because I'd eaten the last samosa, and Venkat 'accidentally' stood on her sari. She always looked a little flushed when she saw a safety pin after that. We always brought flaky samosas and squashed doklas, but my niece is used to being treated to sandwiches and cake. I've brought samosas anyway. I'm not much for cooking, but you can buy them anywhere now. Chicken for me, and lamb for Venkat, his favourite. Little bits of mince stick in my teeth, I try and wash them out with tea.

It's time for the feeding at Penguin Beach. The Humboldt penguins line up like black and white beads on a necklace, while a freshly scrubbed keeper throws fish for them. Some are shy and like to be hand-fed, some are bold and leap into the water as if playing to the crowd. They have cute names like Private and Pingu – I squealed the first time I saw them. Pig-tailed sixteen-year-old me stood here and told Brylcreemed twenty-year-old Venkat that when the freckled girl holding the bucket smiled at me, my tummy fluttered. Looking back, that was probably the last time we talked in full sentences.

We take the first exit, wander into the jellyfish area. These are colourless and stingless, but that doesn't make them less menacing. They float about with no purpose other than feeding and reproducing, and those long tentacles seem made to invade sensitive places. Mummy stood by the left tank and explained that Venkat couldn't join us that year because his wife, who I'd only met at the wedding, was having a hard time with their baby. Daya purses her lips now, pulls them back, mimicking their movement to make me smile.

There's only one more refuge before the confrontation. African dwarf crocodiles watch us with beady eyes, perched on rocks or mostly submerged in murky water. They're vulnerable in the wild, hunted for meat or their habitats destroyed to make way for people, but here it's easy to think they're invincible with their thick, patterned skin. Sometimes people feel their destruction is justified. This is where my father told me Venkat was fighting for custody of Daya, using post-natal depression and rehab visits to build a picture of an unfit mother. I never spoke to her alone, never got to make my own judgement about her. She moved back to Delhi after the court case, one day took an overdose of sleeping tablets. I don't know if that makes Venkat right. I don't know if Daya holds all that inside.

We seem to have synchronised our footsteps; they echo along the walkway. Tap-tap-tap, her clompy trainers and my wedge-heeled boots reverberating with the ancient beat of worn-down loafers, leathery chappals, polished black brogues. They've already started the feeding at the Great Barrier Reef display. We line up for a tub of green salady bits for the green sea turtles, and they chase after chunks of carrot and fronds of lettuce as if this barely disguised tank is the same as entire oceans. The intent expression of a blacktip shark takes me back to when Venkat, secure in his engagement to a girl of good family, explained to me that playing about being attracted to men and women was just me putting off settling down. I only unclenched my hands when bruised lettuce slithered down my wrist. That's when I lost him, when I realised he couldn't see me. I was dead to him first.

Daya's pulling on that wrist now, this pilgrimage has brought the dimples back to her cheeks. I don't know exactly what it's brought back to me, apart from how crumbs of leftover samosas are pervasive. Venkat left most of his money to charity. I didn't expect anything else, but he'd left me his daughter and a lot of random facts about sea creatures, and somewhere in that is trust and acceptance. That's more than enough.

Wind

Turning into the Wind

The Points of Sail
The first few lessons are close to dry land: points of sail, boat positioning. Saira's face becomes smooth and expansive like a calm sea or the face of a little girl who hasn't seen too much.

The headmaster, a slight man with frizzy hair, says there's nothing he can do. A complaint has been made, no contrary evidence has been offered, there's the question of the fees. He looks at a mark on the wide mahogany desk during the whole breath-stealing interview. Saira strides out the narrow gate briskly as if it's not her last day.

Not learning to swim was never a problem until lying in the bath meant having the head forced underwater, lungs burning, breath pushing violently against delicate membranes and thudding eardrums. Trying not to splutter so it wouldn't happen again. It didn't leave a mark, externally.

The text messages start. They're only letters contained inside a screen, small black marks, no substance in the real world. Apart from the knowledge that he has already done all those things.

Getting Underway

Leaving the dock always brought tension and release. The sailing lessons were saltair/clearbreeze/spacetobreathe. Saira's face fresh-scrubbed of worry, her small hand warm against skin. Of course, they were taken away.

The doctor purses her lips. The side of her face has a constellation of moles that form and reform as she squints at the screen. She smells of lavender and antiseptic. At the top of the record, a red triangle blinks. Concerns have already been reported, about erratic behaviour and possible alcohol misuse. They cannot be erased. She doesn't type anything during the appointment, not about the threats, not about the tears. Nothing about the bruises.

Saira's face goes grey before the child contact. Face buried between crooked elbow and curve of waist, she mutters, I don't like it when daddy makes me lie down to take photos. The stomach roils like a sucking vortex opening up on a glass-like lake.

After the court-ordered mediation, there is so much shaking there has to be a place to hide. In the toilets there's a poster – one-in-four women are abused by their partners. Perhaps the thinnest dockline to safety could exist.

Steer with the Tiller

This lesson is supposed to be steering, leaning into port or starboard. Having control over the direction the boat goes, despite how hard the wind pushes back. There's too much time to watch Saira giggle with the breeze shifting her hair into a jaggery-coloured halo and consider how far can a small sailboat go. The wind catches the sail, the boom swings round as if the universe has answered.

The woman on the helpline says leaving the abuser doesn't stop the abuse. For the first time, coercive and controlling behaviour is described, and it's not only fists that leave marks.

There's no sailing this Saturday. There's no sailing anymore. Saira curls up on a scratchy over-stuffed cushion on the floor and flicks through blaring cartoons. The flare of the screen brings back the head slammed against the wall, the hand pressed down on the mouth so hard the teeth pierce the bottom lip. The whispered threats so fierce the eardrums vibrate. Tell anyone about me, and you'll never see Saira again. Shut your mouth in court, or I'll stop paying for your precious sailing lessons. It becomes difficult to sit still; there is pacing. The crack is the oval brass-framed mirror smashing. There must be a culprit, but no one is visible in the fractured glass. Saira doesn't even flinch.

The lawyer is late. When she arrives she's someone different: a tall brunette in clicking kitten-heels with papers spilling out of a very shiny briefcase. She whispers a few instructions, something about sitting up straighter, chin up. She walks like someone who's never been called a whore.

Turning into the Wind

Today it's jibing, turning the stern of the boat through the wind. The boom will shift, there's a need to be aware of position and space and time so no one is knocked off the tiny vessel bobbing in a vast turquoise sea into freezing waters deeper than they can control. Today that might be absolution.

Another helpline call, another woman. The phone is heavy in your dry palm. She says, but you didn't jump overboard, you came up for air, you're the parent holding your child in mind. Would you like to talk through your options?

You lie back in the ceramic bath and list all the ways he has power – money, a new partner, you never reported it, he told the doctor you drink. Lukewarm water laps against your eardrums, sucking your head under, a kind of freedom in feeling the pressure on your face. The balance on the scale against him is one child who has started to wet herself, and a dozen text messages that are only threats because he knows how to make you shrivel.

His lawyer makes accusations of ridiculous threats, of midnight hang-ups and broken car windows that mend themselves before there can be proof. Somehow, this reflects on you, that someone with expensive sandalwood aftershave thinks you're capable of this. The judge's rumpled face is unreadable, which sucks the air out of the room. You keep your eyes ahead, but you're aware of every shift in the currents around you.

Sailing Downwind

You're holding your child in mind when you call, her fresh little face, her brisk walk away from troubles, her curling in on herself. There's no chart to help you when you ring social services to tell them what Saira has told you, but it's something you will do together.

You don't really need the pink elephant armbands now, but they make Saira giggle, and the little eddies of happiness help you float. It's chlorine now, and slapping feet on cold tile, and the bobbing heads of strangers, but somehow worries still become submerged.

Knowing the Answers

In moments of quiet or contemplation, Vetala likes to flitter her wings to announce her presence. I have to disguise my shivers by feigning an itch or adjusting my bangles. Sometimes heads turn, but she's worth it.

I'm about to mix the plaster to start conserving Misty when my old Nokia brick of a phone beeps. I don't like to throw away anything useful. And I don't like to be distracted when I'm working. Vetala's twitching, fluttering through the dead cat in front of me, making the eyelids and whiskers quiver. This time I ignore it all.

Vetala used to be imprisoned on paper until my path brought me to ways she could leap off the page. Recently she's been more active, more engaged. There've been more phone calls and letters. They pile up, or I hang up, and she likes to mark their existence. The Vetala of my childhood didn't know anything about technology; she preferred hills and forests. Not that there are many of those now in Southend, so maybe this interest in communication is her learning to adapt. She does like to dance in the sea breeze when we walk along the pier, while I let the ozone wash away the smell of disinfectant that seeps into the soft places in my skin, the places I haven't toughened up. I tell her the old riddles from the book and new riddles I've found, she shakes herself at those childish conundrums of Nakhpur and Khanpur, and what has two heads and two legs.

I first drew her on those long afternoons at Papa's draughty house in Bishop's Stortford, when I came back from school, and everyone was marooned in a different room. She emerged from my pencil as a finished creature, with long wrinkled wings folded over as she hung from a tree, like the Vetala in the story in Nana's *Baital Pachisi*. She didn't come alive unless she could find a body, but she didn't seem to fit right in people. I tried to find an animal or bird that she could inhabit comfortably, and soon I knew more about mammals than my grandfather, mother and sister wanted to know. We looked the same, Deena and me, but she had neater hair, darker clothes and words were her artform. I stayed quiet through meals, listened to her lisping poems in English and Papa's strident riddles in Hindi, then went to finish shading in a panther until it could leap off the page. Vetala loved that house, with its rows of apple trees, and the timber smell of the distant Portingbury Hills.

Misty is almost finished. I stitch the seam, brush her grey fur to cover it. She was her owner's last joy, his source of wonder and delight. Vetala hides behind the freezer, where I store the animals before preparation. I need her with me, giving these cherished creatures back a breath of life, letting them release a wisp of their spirit, so I can make sure they get back to their humans as recognisable, faithful to their old selves. My hands clench instinctively, jasmine and musk drift through the antiseptic perfection of my tiny office. Deena is here. Vetala remembered before I did that some things cannot be ignored. There's no need for my twin to say again what she thinks of my job, it's there in the line of her shoulders in her neat blue dress, the set of her thin pink lips. This is the niche I made for myself, the only vet on the Essex coast that works with animal burials. Vetala puffs herself up, trying to make herself felt, and I'm not sure who should listen. I look up again, enough to notice Deena's eyes are tired and her earrings don't match.

The drive takes an hour, fresh briny air replaced by the flowery smell of well-tended borders. We roll up the tree-lined drive to the old house, the sloping grey-slate roof speckled with dew. We park in the pristine detached garage, crunch across the gravel path. Deena waits by the front door and takes my hand like the old days when we had something difficult to deal with. We all walk up the winding oak staircase together to my grandfather's bookshelf-lined room, where Deena sprawled comfortably, and I never dared to enter. He's insubstantial, upright in the vast teak four-poster bed, brick fireplace lit on a warm May morning. Vetala breezes straight through me, shakes my veneer of assurance, I blurt out an old riddle.

'What has two heads and two legs, Papa?' Vetala has panicked and disrupted my reception. He'll confuse me with my word-hungry sister, it will be like always – as if I'm not there.

'Scissors, my Gita. I always knew you were listening.' His voice is softer, a zephyr not a gale. His eyes are blurry but focused on the brightly coloured book on the table next to him, Nana's *Baital Pachisi*. Vetala settles on top, folds herself small, starts to disappear inside. 'I want you both to have it, to share it.'

Deena read me the stories from that book before I drew my own. She still holds my hand, I squeeze it gently. Sharing is something I've learnt to do.

Let's Sing All the Swear Words We Know

You're a girl with a bell-shaped nose and an anchor-shaped birthmark. You're Antonia cos it's the closest to the only name your father picked out. You're not the reason he leaves, but you're not enough to make him stay. Your lungs are healthy when nothing else is, and you cry like the rushing river, all deadly undercurrents and no end. You only eat basmati rice and only wear shorts. You tattoo all your Barbies with indelible ink and sing all the swear words your babysitter teaches you in a chant that all the slaps in the world won't knock out. You're a girl with crescent-shaped teeth and your father's kidney-shaped earlobes. You wear grease like perfume and touch every slug. You love the way numbers line up in your head and hide in Maths lessons under your haphazard fringe and your Pearl Jam T-shirts. You're drawn to the smell of heated tarmac and leaves as brown as you under a magnifying glass. Your mouth says 'fuck you' without you having to open it. You're a girl with grapefruit-shaped breasts and a watermelon bottom. You watch the boys as they watch you. You don't have the words to make anyone stay, you talk to yourself when no one's listening. You leave as soon as you can and go back every weekend cos nobody else knows the words to your song.

Love

Monochrome

January

He's standing by the hippos at Byculla Zoo, wiping the sticky mouth of a winsome pig-tailed girl.

She's sitting on a carved wooden bench, coughing, sucking at a slightly damp roll-up.

She follows the tentative strokes of his hand.

He chokes at her chain-smoking and moves away.

February

She's standing by the notice he's trying to read, resplendent in an embroidered teal salwar kamees, holding a gold cigarette holder.

He says, Those things will kill you.

She says, Something's got to.

He likes the way she saunters away.

March

He walks over to where she's waving spoonfuls of aloo chaat at the crocodile lake and puffing at a cheroot, hair up in a messy bun.

She says, Feeling peckish?

He says, The staff said you're here every month.

She says, Just waiting for the new penguin exhibit. And whatever else might show up.

Have you ever seen *Charade?*

April

He's waiting for her outside Byculla station, wearing orange chappals and green shorts, holding a packet of nicotine gum.

She says, You're a rescuer, Zarif, you want to show me how I'm wrong.

He says, I'm a doctor, Prema, that snide tone won't work on me. I'm just thinking of the penguins; they're used to clean air.

She says, I've interviewed Saif Ali Khan, I know a line when I hear one.

And takes the gum.

May

He's eating kulfi with a tiny spoon, she's nosily drinking a Thums Up. Their legs are barely touching.

She says, I bet they miss their air-conditioned chamber.

He says, I expect they miss Chile.

She says raspily, They won't remember it, they'll only remember that Seoul aquarium.

He says, Some things you remember in your bones.

June

They're watching one of the impassive black-headed birds who seems to be staring at nothing.

He says, It's cruel to put publicity over their needs, a tragedy waiting to happen.

She says, Who knows what they need, who knows what *anyone* needs.

He says, What does that say about us?

She spits half-chewed gum into a tissue, leans against a chain-link fence to catch her breath.

She says to the back of his head, Their tongues have spines, nature is cruel, life isn't black and white.

July

He waits for her at the station, but she already knows.

She walks to the exhibit without a word, only her kitten heels clacking insistently.

She makes clicking sounds to the remaining penguins as they huddle in a bedraggled mass, a crowd of well-dressed mourners.

He's loath to interrupt her, not even to say he told her so.

August

He says, We can meet at Sanjay Gandhi Park instead?

She says, To be attacked by monkeys or gawk at tired leopards?

She says, In times of trouble we cleave to what we know.

He says, It's not healthy to dwell.

She says, Not everything has to be healthy to be what you need.

She listens to the dial tone as if it's Mozart.

September

She's slowly moving toward the rhinos, holding a packet of chewdah, her cheeks flushed.

He strides up as if she's trying to get away.

He says, Why didn't you tell me about the COPD? I could have helped you.

She says, But journalism is cut-throat, can you be discreet?

October

He says, I didn't think you were going to pick up.

She says, Your answer was a dandy.

He says, You use words as a weapon.

She says, I take my cues from nature, some of us fight to survive.

The clonking sound of his Dr Pepper can missing his wastepaper basket chimes with her choking breath.

November

She sits on a carved wooden bench by the penguin exhibit, devouring kulfi in chunks that make her teeth hurt.

He stands by a Buddha at Kanheri Caves, wondering who to ask to take his photo.

He pulls his sandwich away from a scavenging monkey.

She wipes at her sticky mouth as she coughs up blood.

December

The white sheet on the hospital bed brings out the inky blackness of her hair.

He says to a passing nurse, No, she's not a patient.

She says to his bowed head, I didn't expect to see you again?

He says, I just wanted to know, why penguins?

She says on an exhale like a bullet fired through water, They have style, they have character.

He sits by the bed, stretches out his hand. They stay there together, not quite touching.

Magic and Candlelight

The ballroom is steeped in the glow from hundreds of candles and tea-lights, transforming the gym into a scene from a Jane Austen. Or any book where shy, proper heroines wait patiently to be asked to dance. Twenty-first-century heroines don't have to rely on chance and whims, Zohra has a plan. She tangles her left hand in her double-layered sage-green dress again, cranes her neck around the interlaced couple in front. Her best friend is late. The soft light has turned the grubby sloping windows mirror-like, Zohra adjusts her updo and rescues the twisted hoop earring trapped in a black curl.

Slight, dimple-chinned Kenneth interrupts her primping, asks her to dance. They're playing a piano version of 'Greensleeves' softly, hopefully just while the gym is filling up. Zohra shakes her head; her dance-card is marked. Kenneth's calves flex as he walks away. Who knew hockey-players had muscles? Alex's calves are lumpy, but she's always been more of a shoulder girl. And that's something she probably shouldn't be thinking about her best friend. She's constantly waiting for Alex, for him to shut down his

Xbox or slick down his hair, there's nothing different about this time. She just wants to know what he finally decided to wear.

As well as the lack of electric light, most of the gym equipment is covered in glittery tapestries worked on all term in art classes. They're all supposed to be in long dresses or fancy jackets. A couple are muttering behind her, about how Regency dresses aren't for everyone, and green looks better with pale skin, not brown. Emmanuel, the other student on the planning committee, twirls past with his boyfriend, both in grey frock coats, black top hats and dark-blue jeggings. Zohra smiles in greeting, gets back a twitchy nod. Emmanuel had pushed for a *Three Musketeers* theme, his mother encouraging his hero-worship of Alexander Dumas because of their shared Haitian heritage. Zohra had kept quiet while Mrs Patterson, the art teacher, waffled on about the fundraiser deserving the magical romantic effect of dressed-up ladies and proper gentlemen. They'd ended up with their tiny Kent school looking like it had been decorated by Tinkerbell in a bad mood and frantic trips to Maidstone to find something to wear. Emmanuel doesn't have much time for people who don't fight for their opinions, but Zohra likes to pace herself.

One of the heads bobbing at the entrance has a flick of hair at the crown and is weaving its way to her. Zohra touches her earrings one more time, adjusts her cleavage. Her older sisters helped her make her outfit after hours looking for pictures of Regency clothes, and it's more low-cut than she's used to. Not that she expects Sudoku-loving, *Fallout*-obsessed Alex to notice. The crowd seems to part a little, she goes up on her toes, hoping to catch a better glimpse. The candle-light shadows his cheekbones into thin slivers, makes his brown eyes into splinters. He's wearing jeans and a black blazer. Green's his favourite colour, she'd hoped they match in some way, and that's definitely why one of those candle-flames has burned its way down her throat and is flickering in her belly. And not because he's holding hands with Trish, the moss-eyed netball captain.

'Couldn't they find any more glitter?' His voice is as warm and smoky as ever, but she tastes ash.

'You're late, Alex. The first dance has almost started. I've got somewhere to be.' Her tongue catches in her teeth, but the words are strong.

Alex raises one eyebrow. 'Why'd you make me write on that card thing if it didn't mean anything?'

Zohra turns over her shoulder as she strides off.

'Something better came up, can't wait for you forever.'

She stomps past the mutterers and hisses, 'There's a West Indian girl in *Sandition*. Brown people weren't just magicked into existence in the 1960s you know.'

There's a space over by the glitteriest fake. She starts to sway, watching her earrings glint in the backlit glass. Emmanuel walks past with something sparkling in a paper cup, and they nod at each other again. This time Emmanuel smiles back.

The Man in the Yellow Shirt

Black ovals
Airports are the worst places to say goodbye; everyone knows this. It's hard-wired in collective psyches, like fear of snakes and lust for sugar. Too many other people, bad lighting, the smell of bleach. So that she lied about plane times and departure gates shouldn't be taken as significant. She rushed through passport control, head down, hand against her pounding heart.

There's a small hawk approaching
The sheaf of papers fluttered in the draft from the door as the bustle intensified in the kitchen. Dinah pressed her sweaty toes into the floor, tilted her head to the static fan. There had to be somewhere in Mangalore with aircon and space for her laptop.

'Mi, I'm going out.'

The compact woman, her emerald sari barely wrinkled by the intense heat of cooking and atmosphere, appeared at the door.

'Be careful, baccha, it's not the same now. You going to meet Harbir, like I told you?'

Dinah was very careful not to bang the screen door.

Only an antelope, no threat

It wasn't the presentation that bothered her, but the act of giving it. She hadn't reconciled to the frustration of working on something, considering the clarity of diagrams and the appropriateness of jargon, the relevance of references and the firmness of conclusions for them not to be noticed. At Bangalore University it had been her neckline; in Arizona it was her accent. Everywhere she went she had seemed to have focused on the wrong sort of tone. If she had something important to say about animal or plant communication, it became easily lost.

A pile of orange fruit

She could go to Pabba's, but the ice-cream parlour held other distractions. Memories, anticipation. The man at the fruit stall looked at her sandals and doubled the price. She walked away on principle, the craving for sweet mango intensified, and there he was.

The slow man in the yellow shirt has a gun

They've avoided two groups of young men playing cricket on the beach, three sandcastles and one group of girls paddling. The salt of the sea mingled with the sweet of the kulfi sellers. She's rejected three different openings: canopy shyness; acoustic communication in moustached bats; did his mother ever forgive her.

'I thought you might come back for the communication conference.' His voice still made her nerve-endings shake, as if they're sending out tiny filaments looking for light.

'Prairie dogs all use the same cry for black ovals, even though they've never seen one before.' She could feel his head tilt from where she studied the way her bare feet left only partial imprints. 'I think that tells you a lot about instinct.'

Sand rubbed at the skin between her toes. He took her hand, which they both knew was the next step. 'Instinct is important.'

Medium-sized rectangles

She dreamt she ate mango ice-cream in Pabba's, blinking at the bright lights and dazzling white tables. In real life it was vanilla, and she didn't notice anything but her term paper. He'd sat down in his custard-apple yellow shirt, asked if she had a spare pen. She looked into deep brown eyes and nothing more needed to be said. The tinkle of spoons in metal bowls became tiny stones rattling against glass. An old ritual from the last time she'd slept in this room.

'Are you awake? I want to show you something.'

His dry hand covered her clammy palm, the night air lifted her hair, brushed gently over her neck and arms. Her toes pressed into red soil, releasing clay and earthiness. He always walked as if the world would wait for him.

Space opened up before them, tiny lights and a huge black rectangle. She'd seen helipads before but not in the middle of nowhere. Something was being said, and she had to find the answer without knowing the question. Prairie dog communication was compact and flexible: alarm calls, food, scenery, indicated with pitch and inflection, able to recognise people from clothing as well as the danger they carried. She'd always admired the way they got a message across.

'Harbir, I didn't go to Arizona because I thought America was better.'

The press of lips against hers was like a chemical release.

The slow man in the yellow shirt

The airport is bigger, flashier, the people louder. Studying how plants and animals convey threats makes her more aware of them. Her cheeks heat up, her eyes can't focus. A woman almost runs over her feet with a chunky silver suitcase, a baby shrieks in her ear, and there he is. Her mouth goes dry. She can't stay, not yet.

He holds up one large smooth hand – a plastic bag of mangos. She smells their intense perfume.

'I would never ask you to stay. Just remember this time, you can come back.'

Their hands touch as she takes the bag, their lips brush. He smells of ink and masala tea, spicy and mellow.

'I always wanted to come back.'

Dinah walks to the gate backwards, ignores tuts of disapproval and squeaks of outraged luggage, so that his face and the yellow shirt are the last things she sees.

Families

Because Someone Else Dances

A scorpion is an opportunist, my grandmother said, as she scrubbed clothes in the bath or peeled potatoes with a knife. Her knuckles were granite bulbs. I didn't know what an opportunist was, but I knew it was a threat, something that came with a sting, like the wasps' nest Nana doused with vinegar and boiling water. It foamed up in vengeance, I drew it with hard loops of scavenged charcoal.

Mother would return from the bank, remove plastic knives from my chubby hands, and say, 'Mumma, can't you learn to use the washing machine?'

I'd be sent off to bed, supposed to be quiet. The voices clashed like the impact of iron against rock, two hard surfaces that shuddered together. I sketched them as massive boulders marooned in an icy sea, looming over a tiny, rudderless boat.

'If I'm good enough to watch her, I'm good enough to teach her. When the well dries up, we realise the value of water.'

The reasons were different, but the words always stayed the same.

My first friend from school, Darren, had very clean white socks that stretched up his calves, and very clean white teeth. I made models of his long-fingered hands in plasticine, like tarantula legs. I asked to bring him to tea. Nana made tiny samosas and chutney sandwiches. She held on to a bottle of vinegar as if it were a talisman. I watched him eat, two or three foodstuffs in his oar-shaped mouth at one time, as if they might disappear. When his lightly stubbled father came to get him, Nana stared at his outstretched hand until he scratched at his neck and walked away.

'Beta,' she said, 'your husband will open you like a ripening fruit, he won't even need to squeeze. Because someone else dances, we do not follow suit.'

She taught me how to chop vegetables in even pieces that day, and how to time the rice from the sound of the steam escaping. We hid the rice-cooker under the stairs, a joke I thought. Mother didn't even notice. And no one laughed.

I was called into the headmistress by mistake. Neela had finally sworn at the boy who pulled her pigtails, and we looked enough alike that our Year 5 teacher sent me instead. She didn't even look up, explained to me boys would be boys, and good girls needed to remember that. Her sideburns were sculpted, like tiny leaves. After that, it was a game. Forgetting my name at the register, looping black graffiti on the netball goal. Why keep the rules of people who thought you were a brown-eyed body with long black hair? My portrait of her became mistletoe winding around a barely grown sapling.

The reasons were different, but the words always stayed the same.

Mother took me to the bank with her, showed me her desk buried under files in a tiny cubicle while she rubbed at the furrow between her brows. She talked about responsibility and promotion opportunities while pushing paperclips into a tidy pile. Nana took me to the market, showed me how to choose the best aubergine, talked about the joys of being a good wife. As she was, to a man who breakfasted on whiskey and sulked if she moved his newspaper.

'Beta,' she said, handing me a bag of finger chillies shedding their intensity even through the paper, 'don't fall at night into the well you saw clearly in the day.'

Dinner was almost silent. I scraped greasy baigan around, Mother's jaw clicked, Nana's bangles rattled. It made me want to fall, or at least jump. I pulled out a slivered chilli and chewed it slowly as it set my tongue ablaze.

I failed A-level art. I'd spent two years filling a portfolio with leafy landscapes, pencilled portraits of film stars, sculptures of women in saris. Unfocused, I was told, no connecting beat. I didn't mention it at home, talked about colleges and universities, buried confusion with cubing paneer as if each piece were art. As the afternoon dissolved into splotches of light, I sorted through discarded scraps of wasp nests and mistletoe, tiny boats and oar-shaped mouths. Fear and Longing, the label written large on the folder as I sent it all off to art school, finally listening to the music I'd always danced to. That evening I noticed how Nana gave me the biggest pieces of chicken tikka, and

Mother opened the daaba of rotis for me, and worked out how I could say goodbye to them both.

And Reverse

Everyone knows that Uno is Mingel's game. His loving older sister has suggested it specially to calm his nerves after the torment of introducing his gentle Hindu girlfriend to his observant Catholic mother. The strategy, the judgement, the yelling – all parts of the future Batchelor of Commerce's skillset. Tonight, everyone knows he's distracted, and they know the reason why.

'Two fours.'

That's Jyoti, hazel-eyed, chubby-fingered, with a smile like a perfectly cut slice of ripe mango. She knows Mingel's distracted because he's realised she wants to drop out of her Batchelor of Education course, flee loud and inhospitable Bangalore where new buildings appear every day, and walk barefoot again through the tea plantations in Munnar. It doesn't mean they won't see each other again, only that not everyone knows what they want to do for the rest of their life when they're twenty years old.

'Skip.'

That's Maria, her sandalwood-scented bluish-black hair closely fitting her like a hood. She knows Mingel's distracted because he caught her sneaking out of the apartment last night. He can't have figured out the reason for the sneaking, the smoking, the sudden interest in random men. The neurologist said she was still in the early stages of MS, and the numbness in her feet and the tingling in her fingers are easily disguised. She holds up the bottle of pink wine, brought for the guest, shrugs at the concert of noes, tops up her own brass-stemmed wine glass with a barely noticeable tremble.

Mingel doesn't seem to notice he's missing a turn. He's replaying the moment he noticed a blue-lined pregnancy test in the bathroom wastepaper basket after dinner. This has replaced the last moment he's been luxuriating in – when he finally lost his virginity five weeks ago, and it made all the snide comments about his virility seem toothless. Jyoti's been different, distant. Could he be a father now and achieve his dreams of opening a chain of luxury coach companies? His devout mother expected better.

'Reverse.'

That's Rakel, mindful of her son, willing him to join in while gnawing on a turmeric-stained thumbnail. She knows Mingel's distracted because he's missing his father, ordered away again to drive the coach on the smooth new road between Bangalore and Mumbai. He'll be back in sixteen hours, enough time for her to prepare her story. Vinesh, her square-chinned first-floor neighbour had teasingly stroked her wrist this afternoon as he returned their newspaper, the way he had stroked between her legs two nights before. She sips her ginger tea, letting the nausea subside. The game is almost over.

Virmala Nagra's Hypotheses on Marriage and Motherhood

Purpose: How to cope with earning more than your husband

Hypothesis: One false step can expose cracks in a nine-year marriage

1. Make sure you remember how he likes his eggs, don't throw away the eggshells (calcium carbonate $CaCO_3$).
2. Put them in his coffee grounds to smooth out the bitterness.
3. Swallow cold tea and the urge to remind him that when he's selling mothballs, they'll be 1,4-dichlorobenzene ($C_6H_4Cl_2$), not flammable naphthalene ($C_{10}H_8$).
4. Laugh at his joke about 'fire in the hold' (fuel + O_2 + heat), don't mention your pay rise, pretend it's fine to stay home with your feisty, red-faced, sweating daughter.
5. After he leaves, add lime to tequila (hydroxy alcohol C_2H_6O) and generously salt (NaCl) the edge.
6. Wonder if the ($C_{10}H_8$) could affect his brain.

Purpose: How to deal with a chemical spill

Hypothesis: A child can sense if your attention is divided

1. Take one screaming, tear-soaked (NaCl) three-year-old.
2. Mop repeatedly.
3. Close your laptop with the unfinished lab report.
4. Eat the lime whole this time; you need the Vitamin C (ascorbic acid $C_6H_8O_6$).
5. Stare at the bottle of C_2H_6O and consider investing in a thermometer containing alcohol for emergencies.
6. Somehow conclude with your husband that if you were more involved, it would all be easier.

Purpose: How to analyse the data from the parent's evening

Hypothesis: Expertise in one area does not transfer to another

1. Sit with your knees together in the skirt you last wore to graduate from Leicester University, feel exposed without your lab coat.
2. Agree that it is fantastic to finally meet Miss Francis, even though she smells like vinegar (ethanoic acid $C_2H_4O_2$).
3. Ignore the stares at your Hello Kitty notebook; you're used to stares.
4. Write carefully that your chubby pig-tailed child eats chalk (calcium carbonate $CaCO_3$) and sand (SiO_2) and screams if she sees green food.
5. Note that pica is unusual, discuss your child's diet: white rice, rice crackers, Laughing Cow cheese, sweet lassi.

6. Theorise that a $CaCO_3$ addiction runs in the family.

Purpose: How to get through the paediatrician's appointment

Hypothesis: A competent parent would be aware if their child was struggling

1. Turn up the corners of your mouth at the revelation that you're both called Dr Nagra.
2. Dream of soaking in a bath full of Epsom salts (magnesium sulphate $MgSO_4 \cdot 7H_2O$).
3. Watch the other Dr Nagra's moustache waggle, think about all the bad things you did as a child, like squash centipedes.
4. Write down: lack of social imagination, difficulty interacting with others, language disorder.
5. Search for an aspirin (acetylsalicylic acid $C_9H_8O_4$) in your canvas shoulder bag. Find instead the picture in Hyde Park, Mandip on his phone, Sarita staring at her fingers.
6. Feel very, very sick.

Purpose: How to tell your husband your child has autism

Hypothesis: The litmus test of a relationship is to put it under pressure and see if it breaks

1. Stare at the bottle of tequila, try and remember when it wasn't an element in your day.
2. Look at the diamond on your fourth finger (Carbon C) and think how much it looks like quartz (silicon dioxide SiO_2), consider if Sarita would eat it.

3. Make a list in your head of all the things that have value because the world decided they do.
4. When your husband arrives, hold out the piece of paper that will change all your lives, warm from your hands (fuel + O_2 + heat).
5. Hear him whisper, 'She's still our feisty girl,' let him mop up your NaCl spill.
6. Remember people are carbon and hydrogen, oxygen and chloride, magnesium and sulphur, and can be infinitely remade.

ACKNOWLEDGEMENTS

Thanks to: Farhana Shaikh for her brilliant Becoming a Writer course, that convinced me that I was one, and to all the brilliant writers that I met through it. Kathy Fish, without whose workshop most of these stories wouldn't have been written. My first readers, Sarah Moola, Nazira Vania and Farhana Khalique. Barbara Byar, who persuaded me to put this collection together and send it out. My Flashback Fiction family for the endless support, the virtual cake and the fisticuffs. And my husband Steve, who always thought this book would exist.

*

The author and publisher wish to thank the editors of the journals in which the following stories were first published:

'What Really Gets You Is the Rising Heat' was first published in *Spelk*, August 2018; 'A Pilgrimage Can Be One Way' – *Bending Genres*, August 2019; 'Various Histories of Sea Serpents' – *JMWW*, October 2018; 'Let's Sing All the Swear Words We Know' – *Lost Balloon*, September 2018; 'Monochrome' – *Open: Journal of Arts & Letters*; 'The Man in the Yellow Shirt' – *Gone Lawn*, December 2018;

'Because Someone Else Dances' – *Rhythm and Bones*, April 2019; 'Virmala Nagra's Hypotheses on Marriage and Motherhood' – *Creative Futures Literary Award Anthology*, October 2018.

SIMILAR TITLES FROM REFLEX PRESS

Some Days Are Better Than Ours
Barbara Byar

'These are searingly truthful fictions. Pitched at the border of poetry and prose, they catalogue lives lived at the edge, survivors facing the beauty and cruelty of the world. These fictions will take your breath away.'
—William Wall, *Suzy Suzy* and *Grace's Day*

'Barbara Byar writes flash like no one else; in each of these lucid and furious twenty-nine stories – some no longer than a single page – are wholly unforgettable glimpses into the lives of her individual characters.'
—Peter Jordan, *Calls to Distant Places*

Some Days Are Better Than Ours is a startling collection that explores human life in all its forms. These stories will make you draw breath as you race through compelling accounts of the dark places people escape to and from.

Through her masterful use of language, Barbara Byar skilfully invites the reader into imagined futures and regretful pasts – from war to childhood to road trips to relationships. Her pieces are visceral, sometimes brutal but sliced through with hope. These stories, and the characters in them, strike straight at the realist heart of the human experience and will linger long after reading.

REFLEX PRESS

Reflex Press is an independent publisher based in Abingdon, Oxfordshire, committed to publishing bold and innovative books by emerging authors from across the UK and beyond.

Since our inception in 2018, we have published award-winning short story collections, flash fiction anthologies, and novella-length fiction.

www.reflex.press
@reflexfiction